The Green Man

Livewire

The Green Man

Sandra Woodcock

JAMESTOWN  PUBLISHERS

a division of NTC/CONTEMPORARY PUBLISHING GROUP
Lincolnwood, Illinois USA

First published in United Kingdom by Hodder & Stoughton
Educational in Association with the Basic Skills Agency.

ISBN: 0-89061-402-4

Published by Jamestown Publishers,
a division of NTC/Contemporary Publishing Group, Inc.
4255 West Touhy Avenue,
Lincolnwood (Chicago), Illinois 60646–1975 U.S.A.
Manufactured in the United States of America.

890 V P 0 9 8 7 6 5 4 3 2 1

CHILLERS

The Green Man

Contents

Chapter   **Page**

The Greens

Eddie was in a bad mood.

It had to do with work.

Things were going wrong.

A job was being held up.

If that happened he lost money.

He hated losing money.

It was all because of a few people.

They were good-for-nothing.

The police weren't doing their job.

That's how Eddie saw it.

It had been a bad job right from the start.

Eddie had won a contract.

He had to clear a building site.

It was for a new shopping center.

There were a lot of trees to clear.

But there was one thing Eddie liked.

If he did the job on time,

he would get a bonus.

At first he thought it would

be easy to get the bonus.

He knew his men would work hard.

But then the trouble started.

People came to save the trees.

They called themselves the Greens.

Eddie called them lots of other names.

They were a funny group.

Some were just kids from the college.

Some were hippies.

There were two old ladies as well.

"They should know better," said Eddie.

The next day more people came.

They were not locals.

They had been on lots of protests.

They knew what to do.

The leader was a tall man with long hair.

His name was Ben.

He wore a T-shirt with a face on it.

It was the face of a green man.

The green man had strange skin.

It was like the bark of a tree.

His hair was like leaves.

The Greens had posters.

The posters said—

SAVE OUR TREES

WE NEED TREES NOT PARKING LOTS.

They shouted at Eddie and his men.

They shouted about birds' nests

and rare plants.

They climbed the trees and sat there.

Eddie's men could not start work.

The TV cameras came.

But nobody moved them.

And Eddie was losing money.

Eddie Loses His Temper

The Greens lived on the site.

They stayed there day and night.

Some slept in tree houses.

After three days Eddie lost his temper.

He yelled at the police.

"Do something. They are breaking the law!

Can't you move them?"

The police said they had to be careful.

"We can't take any risks.

Things can get out of hand.

People can get hurt. They could get killed.

Give us time," they said.

But it was all too slow for Eddie.

He made up his mind to do something.

"You can start tomorrow," he told his men.

"What are you going to do?" they asked.

But Eddie would not tell them.

He was busy thinking.

He didn't speak to anyone.

His men saw the look on his face

and kept away from him.

Eddie went home.

His wife was watching the TV.

"Hey Eddie!" she shouted.

"There's that Ben from the site.

He's on the TV news."

Someone was asking him about his T-shirt.

"Who was the Green Man?"

"He is the old spirit of the woods," Ben said.

"He is the keeper of Nature.

People have always believed in him.

We keep his spirit alive today.

We try to look after Nature."

"Turn the TV off," said Eddie.

"I have work to do.

I have to sort out the men's wages.

Don't wait up for me."

Eddie's wife could take a hint.

"I'm off to bed then," she said.

She went up the stairs.

She could hear Eddie looking

for something in the kitchen.

Then everything was quiet.

"He's up to something," she said to herself.

3

The Plan

Eddie left home at midnight.

He didn't take his car.

He wanted to be very quiet.

He didn't want the Greens to hear him.

It had not rained for weeks.

So in the woods it was very dry.

Eddie was going to start a fire.

Then the Greens couldn't stay in the trees.

The fire would drive them out.

Eddie found a big can of gasoline.

It was near one of his trucks.

He took it out.

He crept towards the trees.

It was very still. The moon was bright.

He looked into the trees.

He could see dark shapes.

They were the Greens. They were asleep.

4

No Escape

Eddie crept under the trees.

There was no sound.

He poured gasoline on the grass.

It was very dry.

He took out a match. Then he stopped.

He saw a big shape coming towards him.

The shape seemed to come from a tree.

At first Eddie thought it was Ben.

The dark shape came closer.

It looked too wild to be a person.

The blood drained from Eddie's face.

His legs felt like jelly.

The big shape came closer.

It seemed to have hair like branches.

The face was lined and twisted.

It was like the face of an old tree.

It was tall, much taller than Eddie.

His mouth went dry.

He started to shake.

He dropped the gasoline can and began to run.

His feet slipped on the dry grass.

He tried to scream but

no sound came out.

Behind him he heard a thump, thump, thump.

It was the heavy feet of a monster.

He heard the thump of his own heart.

Now it was hard to breathe.

He couldn't go on.

He fell to the ground and

turned his head to have one last

look behind him.

5

The Look of Fear

The next morning the police came.

They found Eddie's body.

They saw the gasoline can.

The grass smelled of gasoline.

They knew what Eddie had tried to do.

The people in the trees began to wake up.

They came down and looked at Eddie.

No one had seen him in the night.

No one had heard him.

They were shocked by the gasoline.

They knew what he had been doing.

Ben, the leader, stepped forward.

He looked at Eddie's face.

It was frozen with a look of fear.

"Not a pretty sight," he said.

He took off his T-shirt.

It had the Green Man on it.

He bent down and put it over Eddie's face.